BUNNIES AT CHRISTMASTIME

Pictures by Marie H. Henry / *Story by* Amy Ehrlich

Dial Books for Young Readers / New York

For Lizzie. Merry Christmas!
A. E.

To Frederique, Clo, Maïca
M. H. H.

First published in the United States 1986 by
Dial Books for Young Readers
2 Park Avenue
New York, New York 10016
Originally published by Duculot, Paris-Gembloux 1986
Published simultaneously in Canada by
Fitzhenry & Whiteside Limited, Toronto
© 1986 by Duculot Paris-Gembloux
© 1986 by Amy Ehrlich for the American text

Printed in Belgium by Offset Printing Van den Bossche
Typography by Nancy R. Leo
First Edition
COBE
2 4 6 8 10 9 7 5 3 1

Library of Congress Cataloging in Publication Data
Henry, Marie H.
Bunnies at christmastime.
Translation of: Et si on invitait le père Noël?
Summary: An invitation to Santa Claus to join the
bunnies for a Christmas party brings their Uncle Jack
instead, but he comes with toys and Santa whiskers.
[1. Rabbits—Fiction. 2. Christmas—Fiction.
3. Santa Claus—Fiction.]
I. Ehrlich, Amy, 1942– . II. Title.
PZ7.H395Bvt 1986   [E]   86-2202
ISBN 0-8037-0321-X

The full-color artwork was prepared using pencil and
watercolor washes. It was then camera-separated and reproduced
as red, blue, yellow, and black halftones.

It was Christmas Eve, a lovely snowy day. Mother Bunny sent her children to the village to do some errands.

"Stop at Uncle Jack's and remind him about the Christmas party," she said. "He's been so absentminded lately."

"You can count on us," said Paulette. She was the oldest.

But the moment Mother Bunny was out of sight, Larry and Harry started acting up. Paulette stood it as long as she could. Little brothers were the worst!

"How much farther? How much farther?" they kept asking all the way to Uncle Jack's house.

"Come on," said Paulette. "We'll be there in a minute."

But what was this? No one answered.   At last the bunny children gave up...

and headed for the village.

Suddenly they heard singing and clapping. Paulette could hardly believe her eyes. There, on the main street…

could it be?
Yes, it was.
It was Santa Claus!

Paulette walked right up to him. "Merry Christmas, Mr. Santa."

"Want to come to our Christmas party?" asked Harry.

"It's tonight," said Larry.

"If you come, we'll have cake." "With strawberries?" asked Santa.

"Yes, with strawberries!" said the bunnies. "I'll be there for sure," Santa promised.

"Mama, Papa!" shouted the bunny children. "Guess who's coming to our Christmas party!"

"Uncle Jack?" asked Mother Bunny.

"No, Santa Claus! Can we make him a cake, Papa? A *strawberry* cake? Please say yes, Papa!"

"Children, children, calm down," said Mother Bunny.
"Let your father have his tea."

At last Mother and Father Bunny were ready to help with the baking.

Hurry up, bunnies!
On your mark!
Get set...
Go!

And the cake was ready
in no time flat.

Oh, no!

Next came the Christmas decorations.

"Don't cry, Paulette," said the bunny brothers. "You can put up the star."

But in the end, *everyone* put up the star.

"Which stocking are you going to hang?" asked Harry.

"Let's take both and our shoes besides. That way we'll get more presents," Larry said.

It sounded like a good idea to Paulette.

She couldn't figure out why Larry and Harry were annoyed.
It wasn't *her* fault she had more shoes than they did.

"Hurry, children," said Mother Bunny. "Someone's at the door."

It was Grandma and the bunny cousins. Paulette, Larry, and Harry rushed to tell them the news. "Santa's coming! Santa's coming!" they cried.

"Maybe this is Santa now," said Mother Bunny.

But it was only
Uncle Jack. Hey,
wait a minute!
Something strange
was going on....

First Uncle Jack disappeared into the other room.

Then he asked for his bag.

Quietly, oh, so quietly, the bunny cousins tiptoed to the door and opened it a crack.

What they saw was unbelievable.

Truly amazing!

Suddenly the door swung open.

"Are you Uncle Jack or are you Santa Claus?" the bunny cousins asked.

"I will tell you this," he said. "Tonight on Christmas Eve I am Santa. Now let the party begin!"

"Deck the halls with boughs of holly!

Fa la la la la

la la la la."

"Presents, presents! Presents for all the good little bunnies!" cried Santa. It was the moment they had been waiting for.

There was music...

and dancing...and good times for all.

In the end only Larry was still awake to say good-bye to Santa.
"Will you come to our party again next year?" he asked.
"I would be honored," said Santa.
Then he picked up Uncle Jack's bag and walked away.

BUNNIES
ALL DAY LONG

BUNNIES AND
THEIR GRANDMA

"Two homey and quietly droll books about the Bunny family. The author's inspiration are color pictures crackling with energy."

Publishers Weekly

"Books both children and adults will love reading and looking at...Amy Ehrlich's *Bunnies* books tell warmly and with humor about the everyday activities of the Bunny family, particularly the three children of the family. Ehrlich writes simply and naturally, capturing the talk of typical children. Henry's illustrations are soft, warm, and wonderfully funny in their depiction of the bunnies playing, arguing, causing trouble."

Children's Book Review Service

"*Bunnies All Day Long* and *Bunnies and Their Grandma* are an appealing pair of companion books by Amy Ehrlich with pictures by Marie Henry. The line-and-wash illustrations are pastel...and include some touches of humor. The texts—the cycle of a family day, going to a party at Grandma's house—have the appeal of everyday life and are written in a light and lively style."

Chicago Tribune, Zena Sutherland